# DRAKE SCIENCE FICTION PRIVATE EYE SHORT STORIES COLLECTION

CONNOR WHITELEY

No part of this book may be reproduced in any form or by any electronic or mechanical means. Including information storage, and retrieval systems, without written permission from the author except for the use of brief quotations in a book review.

This book is NOT legal, professional, medical, financial or any type of official advice.

Any questions about the book, rights licensing, or to contact the author, please email connorwhiteley@connorwhiteley.net

Copyright © 2021 CONNOR WHITELEY

All rights reserved.

# DEDICATION
Thank you to all my readers without you I couldn't do what I love.

## A FAMILY MAILING AFFAIR

"Blackmail is about pressure, always remember that,"

-Former Grand Arbiter of the Human Empire

There was something about blackmail cases that Drake loved, he didn't know exactly why off the top of his head. It was probably because some were extreme, some were meh and others were clever.

Sitting in his favourite red leather booth with a black metal table and another dirty red leather chair in front of him, Drake was really looking forward to this meeting.

A part of him guessed it was good he didn't get many blackmail cases as a Private Eye but it was a shame. They did pay well. Drake smiled as he remembered his standard rate for these sort of cases were about a thousand credits plus expenses incurred.

Listening to the loud jazz music of the bar, Drake relaxed and pressed his back into the soft, cold leather chair and he rested his hands on the colder metal table.

He wanted to wave his hand over to one of the blue holographic servants that looked perfectly female, but Drake was comfortable. Focusing on the holographic servants he knew they were customised for the male crowd. Yet they did nothing for him.

Stretching his neck a little, Drake looked to the far end of the bar past all the young people dancing and to the counter with all the drinks. Drake smiled and wished he could go over there and talk to the barman. His long smooth brown hair and quick moves for making drinks was hot.

Changing his attention to the loud music and the people dancing on the black dance floor with the disco lights flashing around, Drake was expecting himself to question why his client wanted to meet here. But from what he knew about the client this was a perfect spot. Quiet, discrete and a place few proper people came to.

Definitely not Drake's scene but that's another part of the job he loved, he got to travel the Human Empire and see new cultures. (And new men)

Seeing something out of the corner of his eye, Drake turned his head to see a tall muscular man taking a seat on the red leather chair. His long business black suit was strange for a place like this. Even his hair was smooth and perfectly placed. If Drake wasn't on a job, he might have found the guy attractive, but something felt off. The man checked over his shoulder.

"Drake?" he asked, his voice concerned and

deep.

"Heron Drake, Private Eye authorised by the Agents of The Emperor," Drake said, his voice full of authority.

The client checked over his shoulder again.

"Um I didn't know Private Eyes counted as Agents of the Emperor,"

Drake nodded. "We are somewhat further down on the list of important people but we have some powers,"

He checked over his shoulder.

"If you're wondering if you're being followed. You are not. There is no one watching us,"

"Are you sure?" he said, clearly tense.

"What's going on?" Drake asked.

"I'm being blackmailed,"

Drake wanted to roll his eyes. "Please know everything will be okay. Just tell me what happened. I'm here for you,"

The client seemed to relax a little bit. Drake smiled at him.

"I've been getting letters for a week now demanding too much money. I don't have the money. They can't tell my secret!"

Drake gestured for the man to calm down and take a few breaths.

"Who are you?" Drake asked, remembering that was always useful. He checked earlier of course but he had forgotten now.

"I'm sorry. Were are my manners. I am Judge Ozzi of the Arbiters,"

Drake nodded remembering the name from the case file. Judge Ozzi. A great man. A man who believed in justice and the betterment of society. A part of Drake wanted to help this judge no matter what happened. But he still needed to be careful and get paid.

"I'm being blackmailed for a horrific crime. Something appalling. I didn't even do it,"

As the Judge continued to stress how disgusting it was and how he was innocent of this crime, Drake couldn't help but wonder what it was. Killing a child? Kidnapping? Rape?

"They're saying I'm... I'm gay," the Judge said.

Drake was glad he didn't have a drink at the moment. He would have choked. Instead he just stared at the judge. A great man? Drake rolled his eyes.

He couldn't understand how a judge like Ozzi who had given serial killers lighter sentences on the condition they're rehabilitated. (and it worked) Then he hated gays.

In all the news reports, Drake had seen Ozzi was presented as the candidate and poster boy for change and progress. Clearly they were lies.

"What's your fee?" the judge asked.

"Three thousand," Drake said, if he was going to have to save a homophobe he might as make money out of it.

"Of course that's very fair. Thank you,"

"Do you know who the blackmailer is?" Drake asked, sometimes it paid off.

Ozzi smiled. Drake was disgusted by it all his teeth were so perfect and white. They were too perfect. It was unnatural.

"My blackmailer dear Drake is…"

Drake frowned as he saw Ozzi's eyes widen and they turned watery.

"My blackmailer is my son. Please excuse me," Ozzi said, as he walked away.

Watching that horrible Ozzi walk away, Drake couldn't help but wonder what was the full story. A son doesn't just blackmail their own father without a good reason. Nor does a judge of the Arbiters get so scared over a little rumour especially about being gay. That was a normal now. No one cared if you were gay or straight.

So what was going on?

\*\*\*

Feeling the hot air blow past him as the hot wind and flying cars flew past, Drake leant against the hard black metal railings of a metal bridge.

Drake watched all the flying cars in all their different shapes, sizes and classes rush past on the road below him. It was one of the most travelled routes in the entire city.

Turning around, Drake smiled as he watched the handful of people on the bridge walk past doing their daily business. Judging from their clothing they were office workers probably coming from the legal firm on one side of the bridge. Then they were walking to the train station on the other side of the bridge. But being here was what Drake needed for this job.

Breathing in the harsh recycled air of the city and admiring the tens of lights on the futuristic buildings either side of him, Drake started to think about why the son would be blackmailing his father. It was odd. In all his years as a Private Eye, this was the first blackmail case that involved family.

Drake had wanted to call his friend Petic, another Private Eye, to see if she had encountered this before. But Petic was busy with court cases on Earth sadly.

Looking at the large glass entrance of the legal firm, Drake's eyes narrowed as he tried to see if the son was coming out. His research had clearly showed the son worked here as a top lawyer. Was he late finishing work?

Just as Drake was about to walk into the legal firm and request to see the son (maybe his name was Rubio, Drake wasn't sure), a tall young man walked out in a well-fit tight black suit. He was about the same age as Drake. Probably very late twenties. Drake couldn't help but he smiled as Rubio walked out.

As Rubio walked across the bridge, Drake had to admire his long confident strides and his short blond hair that framed his square face perfectly. Rubio looked at Drake and smiled.

"Rubio," Drake said.

Rubio stopped but his eyes narrowed and his eyebrows lowered.

"I'm Heron Drake, Private Eye,"

Rubio rolled his eyes and laughed for a moment.

"My father?"

Drake nodded and gestured Rubio to step to one side. He did. Drake followed and leant against the cold hard metal wall.

"So he finally guessed I was blackmailing him," Rubio said, his voice young, beautiful and perfect.

Drake wasn't sure what to say.

"Is he going to pay me?"

"I don't think so. Please forgive my questions but I don't understand this. Why do it?"

Rubio didn't answer. Instead he just gave Drake a perfect beautiful smile.

"I researched you, your sister, mother and father. You all seem fine. No public arguments. I'm suspecting your parents will be divorcing but that's a good thing judging by my research,"

Rubio nodded. "You're right about the divorce. They're both excited about their new lives,"

Drake smiled. At least he got him talking.

"Why blackmail your father? Why risk a capital offence?"

"I too do my research Mr Drake. I was certain he would go to you. It wasn't hard to manipulate the search results of his computer,"

Drake gave a nervous laugh.

"You wanted me on the case?"

Rubio nodded. "Yes, you remember what a horrible man my father is,"

"You knew I was gay and... what?"

"I knew you wouldn't accept my father calling us names and explaining how horrific we are,"

"Us?" Drake asked.

A loud flying car bombed past. Drake frowned knowing that person would get a large fine for speeding.

"Let me get this straight. You're gay. You're blackmailing your father for revenge? Because he hates you,"

"My father thinks I'm straight. Otherwise he's threatened to kill me. I want the money so I can leave this planet and live my life,"

Drake smiled as he got this answer and understood what the beautiful Rubio meant. It wasn't uncommon for people to run away from people who hated them. Drake nodded as he had done exactly the same after his military service of five years.

A part of Drake wanted to drop the case or help Rubio but he needed to get paid. Drake couldn't drop clients out the blue when their morality was questionable. He would be out of clients.

Another part of Drake wanted to forget that Rubio had said about the threats and he was living in constant fear. He had a job to do. He had to do it.

What if there was a third option?

"What secret are you using against your father?"

Rubio smiled.

"The reason for the divorce. Your father's... he wouldn't be gay. That goes against his character. He's what? Bi?"

Rubio nodded. "And to him that's okay because he still likes women. He still prefers them,"

"But you're a disgusting thing that needs to die?" Drake asked.

More people started to cross the bridge as it was approaching the height of rush hour. The trains would be packed now.

"I need to get paid. Can I convince you to not blackmail your father?"

Rubio laughed. "No. I need to escape. I cannot live under the threat of death anymore,"

Drake shook his head. This was all so ridiculous. He had to help Rubio get away from his family, but he had to get paid as well.

Admiring Rubio's beautiful smooth youthful face and his amazing hair, Drake realised there might be away so everyone could get what they wanted, even himself. Maybe nothing needed to be done except talk. Before he organised that though, Drake needed to make a phone call to Earth.

But the only question was- would Drake get paid and Rubio when this was all over?

\*\*\*

Returning to the bar, Drake allowed the soft red leather booth to mould to his body as he sat down.

Rubio still in his amazing well fitting black suit sat next to him. Drake couldn't help but smile at that.

Breathing in the sweat filled air from the youth on the dance floor who were still dancing, or maybe it was a new crowd. The taste of salt formed on his tongue which made him remember himself as a partying teenager in all the best clubs on Earth.

Drake looked at the far end of the bar past all the people to the counter where the hot barman was. As Drake looked at him and admired his amazing long smooth brown hair, he realised he wasn't as amazing as it once was. In fact, Drake didn't feel that drawn to the barman.

But as he looked at a very nervous Rubio, Drake couldn't help but feel excited and a bit like a teenager once more. Even his hands were sweating at the sight of Rubio.

Listening to the loud jazz music of the bar along with the constant drunk laughter and shouting of the youth, Drake knew his plan had to work. He was sure if Ozzi and his son talked. This would all be sorted.

Then his stomach twisted in a knot as he tried to think about what would he do if it didn't. As a private eye, he was loyal to his client and the person who paid him. He needed those three thousand credits the Judge would pay him. He couldn't just throw away the money because he liked Rubio.

Still a part of him felt like he had to do something about the Judge, it wasn't right a someone who hated gays that much and wanted to kill their own son to get out of this perfectly fine.

It didn't take much longer for Judge Ozzi to finally join Drake and Rubio. Drake frowned at the Judge as he saw the Judge's awful long sterile white robes of power. But what concerned Drake was he noticed the Judge was holding a small black pistol.

"Relax Drake the pistol isn't for you," Ozzi said, his voice cold.

Drake frowned. He rested his arm on the cold metal table. Placing it firmly in front of Rubio. He couldn't let anything happen to him.

"I see you didn't kill him," Ozzi said.

Drake's eyes narrowed. "I was never going to kill a blackmailer. He's your son-"

Ozzi pointed at Drake. "That thing is not my son,"

Drake smiled. "Really. You're a Judge known for progress and innovation. Why do you hate gays so much? You're Bi,"

Ozzi's eyes narrowed and his fingers tighten around the trigger of the pistol.

"I'm confused. I don't want to be like this. I want to help my son correct himself,"

Drake laughed at the Judge. This was so stupid, so pathetic.

"Listen here Ozzi. Your son won't blackmail you anymore so pay me," Drake said, firmly.

Ozzi looked at Drake intensely. "No,"

Drake leaned a little closer. "We had a legally

binding verbal agreement. You pay me three thousand credits for the job,"

"But you didn't do the job. And as you said I am the Judge of Progress and Innovation. No one will question me if I have you arrested,"

Rubio let out a little gasp.

Drake laughed for a brief moment and leant back into the soft red leather booth.

"You know I made a phone call to my good friend Petic on Earth. She told me something very interesting about a new law. The transmissions are still travelling throughout the Empire but it's now perfectly legal for a child to take money from their parent's accounts if their life is in danger,"

Ozzi shook his head.

Rubio leant forward. "It means father I'm leaving. You can't hurt me anymore,"

Drake looked at Rubio unsurely about what he said. Then in the flashing light of the bar, Drake saw some bruises coming out of his amazing tight shirt collar.

"And Ozzi just imagine the embarrassment you'll face if people find out you abuse your own son. Wait until I talk to your daughter," Drake said.

Ozzi let go of the little pistol and frowned.

"What do you two want?" he asked.

"I want my four thousand credits," Drake said.

Ozzi looked like he was about to protest but he went silent.

"And I want ten thousand credits. I am leaving,"

Rubio said.

Ozzi got out a blue holographic phone and swiped the screen before he left. Drake didn't need to see his account to see the money had been transferred. After years as a Private Eye, Drake knew what a man out of thousands of credits looked like. Ozzi wasn't happy.

Watching Rubio check his account on his yellow holographic phone, Drake couldn't help but feel a little happy. Today he hadn't just helped a client get rid of a problem. But Drake had actually made a difference to the Empire today.

Of course Drake knew it wasn't a dramatic difference and it was hardly going to change the fate of mankind. But he had helped an innocent person escape abuse.

Breathing in more of the sweat filled air and listening to the partying youth, a part of Drake still wanted to go out with Rubio so, so bad. He wanted him. But Drake tried to force those thoughts out of his mind. They were inappropriate, surely? He was the client's son. Wouldn't it be bad for business?

With Rubio laughing adorably to himself over how much money he had in his account, Drake couldn't believe how happy he was. Rubio was finally going to escape his family. Drake knew how good that felt.

He kissed Rubio's head.

After realising what he had done, Drake stopped

and gave Rubio an embarrassed look. Rubio kissed him back. Hard.

Feeling Rubio's soft lips against his, Drake felt so lucky to be alive and he learnt a very important lesson today. Something he would use in the future. Blackmail was always about finding pressure. So Drake needed to find pressure of his own. Petic had helped this time but he might need to help himself next time.

Giving Rubio a final deep kiss, Drake grabbed his soft hand and they both left. Ready to escape from this world and maybe start a new adventure together.

# DEFINING CRIMINALITY
"A truly criminal act is something that only harms society,"

-Arbiter of Mercury

Assignments are always fun for private eyes. So maybe that's why Drake loved them so much. Assignments were so interesting and varied because some of them were simply getting dirt on someone for a petty argument between businesses. Or they could be a lot more interesting. Drake hoped this time was the latter.

Feeling the little chrome metal bench take his weight and the icy coldness of it shoot up his spine, Drake knew this was going to be an assignment well worth his time. If only for the view outside the large glass window that made up an entire wall of the brown room he was in.

Looking around the large brown room, Drake had to give the blade-like transport ship some credit. Because all the large round washing machines were perfectly silent and looked like they had been embedded into the walls. Even all the tiny buttons and lights on the machines were perfectly clean.

The only sounds Drake could hear was the slight hum of the bright lights in the ceiling and the quiet noise of people talking in the rooms above and below him.

This entire washing room was shockingly perfect compared to some of the washing rooms on other ships. Some looked like a child had thrown washing machines into the wall and left them there. They were normally that dented and unloved. It was almost like the owners of the ships didn't think people needed to wash their clothes. At least this ship had good machines.

Turning his head, Drake was rather surprised that even the white and black titled strips on the floor were clean. Drake shook his head at how weird this washing room was compared to all the others. He had even spent time in apartments that weren't as clean as this.

Looking out the window Drake smiled as he watched all the amazing stars in the distance and the massive blue planet with white swirling clouds below slowly past the large blade like transport ship he was on.

As much as Drake hated travelling economy class, when it was for a client he didn't mind. And as his mother said it was always good to remember how others lived. But judging by the dirty people he had seen who wouldn't know good hygiene even if it hit them in the face, Drake knew exactly why he travelled first class.

Remembering what his client (the grieving parents of a missing daughter) had said, Drake scanned the washing room for his target or person of interest. But they weren't here just yet.

The smell of washing powder, that reminded him of his university days on Earth with his massive amounts of washing to do, made Drake look back at the machines.

If someone had walked in at that moment, Drake wouldn't be surprised if they thought it was weird he was alone waiting for his washing to be done. In the past two hours, he had only seen two other people but they weren't his target. He needed to meet her.

A part of Drake thought it was weird the client wanted him to talk to a Mrs Sarah Oddballa for information on a disappearance in the main mining town on Raptic 5, a nearby mining world. But the money looked good so Drake didn't mine.

Drake allowed a small smile to break out on his face as he remembered all the stories of the crime lords on Raptic 5 and how they would use the mines for *creative business purposes*. He had no idea if they were true or not. But they were good stories.

The sound of the five women laughing and talking as they walked into the washing room made Drake carefully turn to face his target.

He had finally found Sarah Oddballa.

It was stupid that Drake had had to hunt high and low for her in the kitchen, dining area and now the washing room. But at least the hard work had finally paid off.

Looking subtly at Sarah Oddballa, Drake understood why the client had thought of her as attractive. Her strong long brown hair was perfectly straight running down her long back. Even her posh business suit seemed to be perfectly pressed. Despite her probably just finishing a hard day's work.

But that was something Drake couldn't understand. What was her job? He had tried to find out. He had scanned entire databases as research and Drake had even called his private eye friend Petic on Earth to find out. Still, there was nothing on Oddballa.

Watching Oddballa's long arms carefully and elegantly throw her shirts, dresses and other clothes into a machine. Then she sprinkled in some bright pink sweet smelling washing powder. She looked at Drake.

That wasn't a good sign.

Drake turned to watch the stars in the far distance through the window. But he heard the typical tapping of high heels get closer to him.

A part of him would love to have his boyfriend Rubio here to help him. Maybe Drake would invite him next time. Having a boyfriend here would provide a sexy distraction and cover for him. But it looked like his cover was blown now.

"Heron Drake?" Sarah Oddballa asked, her voice posh and had a thick French accent.

Drake's eyes widened. Turning around Drake smiled and his face turned to confusion as he saw the woman taking a seat next to him.

"Do not pretend you aren't Heron Drake. How

is Rubio?"

Drake's eyes widened at that. How did she know about his boyfriend?

"Heron Drake, I do my research. I can tell you there are twenty undercover Arbiters on this ship and two assassins. I know when there are threats nearby,"

Drake didn't know what to say. He had met clever, dangerous people before, but her words didn't seem dangerous or threatening. They seemed more matter of fact.

"I'm impressed Sarah. May I call you Sarah?" Drake asked.

Oddballa nodded.

"I didn't know you were this well informed," Drake said, deciding this woman might be easier to talk to if she didn't see him as a threat.

"When you do what I do for a living, being well-informed keeps you alive. I've been looking out for people like you since you were born,"

Drake cocked his head.

"Heron, may I ask who hired you?"

"Sorry, I'm never going to say that. My clients-"

"Heron, your client is probably a fake. But I like principled people. Ask me your questions? Be quick please I only did a quick wash,"

Drake nodded and looked behind Sarah to see the other people she had walked in with were all talking to themselves quickly. Like they didn't even know Sarah was missing or Drake was there.

"Raptic 5. There was an incident there and you know something about it,"

Oddballa smiled. "Mr Drake, you are investigating a crime?"

Drake paused before nodding. "Someone disappeared so yes. That would have to be a crime,"

"Why Heron?"

"It's against the law to kidnap or kill someone. If someone goes missing that is what normally happens,"

"I agree Heron, but what if there wasn't a crime?"

"Then I wouldn't be here. My client would have no need to hire me,"

Sarah nodded like she knew exactly what Drake was saying. Drake was a bit unnerved by her.

"What happened to the young woman on Raptic 5?" Drake asked.

"Heron, for your own good I would leave this alone. Or check if your client is who they say they are?"

"I didn't become a Private Eye yesterday. I do know to trace every account and payment I receive. It checked out,"

An intense wave of sweet lavender washing powder filled the air as one of the other women started their washing.

"Did you check where the money came from Heron?"

Drake ignored her. "Tell me what happened and

I can leave you in peace,"

She laughed. "Oh Heron, I think you're the first person to ever say that to me. Normally when people find me they want to kill me,"

"Who are you? What do you do?"

Oddballa's eyes narrowed and she gave Drake a warning look.

"I'm sorry. I shouldn't have asked. What happened to that young woman? Her name was-"

"Anabolic Lex. Aged 23 standard earth years. No boyfriend or girlfriend. Worked as a… caretaker for the mining town. My dear Heron, I said I do my research,"

As Drake heard some of the women laugh, he really started to wonder who was the real Sarah Oddballa. He hadn't met anyone so through and obsessed with research.

"So you know her. She went missing two months ago. The local Arbiters didn't find anything. But witnesses said you were there,"

Sarah pointed her finger up before gesturing Drake to be quiet.

"Heron, you're sadly misinformed. The local Arbiters didn't want to find anyone,"

Drake leant closer. "Why?"

"My research shows you're a military man Drake. Navy,"

Drake laughed for some reason and nodded. Was there anything this woman didn't know?

"Well Drake, you must have known when orders come from high up. You do not disobey them,"

Drake nodded as he started to understand.

"Caretaker. She wasn't a caretaker. She was a fixer. Which Crime Lord?"

Sarah smiled and nodded. "Now you're starting to understand, Drake. Why do you think she was only loyal to one Crime Lord?"

"She was a fixer for all of them. Rare. Interesting but rare. I'm guessing she's well and truly dead then. Killed for a transgression against the Crime lords?"

"Now, now Heron. I will not tell you that. But just know there will be a lot less broken fingers and bodies now Anabolic is disappeared,"

Drake wondered for a few moments if this Sarah Oddballa (if that was her real name) had killed her. It was possible. Sarah seemed like the assassin type. But was that just reaching a bit too far?

One of the washing machines beeped several times.

"My dearest Heron, is there anything else? My washing is almost done,"

Drake wanted to keep her here but he had already been paid and he had what he needed. Sarah had told him Anabolic was a fixer who had probably been killed by one of the Crime Lords on Raptic 5 for a transgression. That was enough. It was enough for her grieving parents to know. If that's what they wanted to know.

"Yes that is all Sarah Oddballa. Thank you for

speaking with me. If you ever-"

Sarah gave him a friendly smile. "Mr Drake, this is not the last time we will be seeing each other. Mark my words,"

Drake's mouth dropped slightly as he watched Sarah walk back over to her friends. Within seconds she was laughing, talking and enjoying her time with her friends like nothing had ever happened. It was like she had never left.

As Sarah pulled her clothes out of the washing machine, Drake breathed in the sweet washing powder she had used. But he still couldn't help but be a little disturbed by the whole encounter. Sarah Oddballa had known everything about him. She probably knew everything about Rubio too. It was weird but he felt knowing what Sarah Oddballa was, wasn't worth the risk. Maybe he would let this one go. Not every question needed to be answered.

Listening to the quiet hum of bright lights, Drake smiled as he wondered what Rubio was doing up in their little silver apartment on the ship. Drake really wanted to go back up there and run his fingers through Rubio's short blond hair and admire his stunning beauty.

Standing up and pulling his clothes out of the washing machine, Drake wondered about a point Sarah had made about if the disappearance (murder) of Anabolic was a crime.

He had no doubt she was a criminal who hurt a

lot of good people. He had met enough fixers as a Private Eye to know the type. So maybe this wasn't a crime. Maybe this was a good thing. Maybe he just needed to accept Anabolic wasn't a crime. After all, true crimes are only things that harm society. And Anabolic's death hardly hurt anyone. Especially if her parents weren't who they said they were.

# THE MARTIAN AFFAIR

"Getting Dirt is easy. Knowing what to do with it is harder,"

-Old Earth Saying, Unknown Region

It was rare for Drake to accept assignments and cases that required him to dig up dirt on other people. It wasn't that he didn't like them, Drake actually found them great fun. But sometimes they were far below his skill set. He really hoped this one wouldn't be.

As he stretched his aching muscular back, Drake had to look away from his light blue holographic computer screen for a moment.

Leaning back on his soft cushioned chair, Drake stared up at the ceiling for a moment and he smiled at that stunning view. It was beautiful. It was really beautiful as Drake watched the bright night stars of far away solar systems twinkle and shine like little beacons in the darkness.

But what was even more beautiful was the stunning array of ships high in orbit. The tall grey blade like ships and much larger warships were stunning to watch. Drake loved all their lights that flashed, and all the thousands of fighters and supply shuttles zoom in and out.

Considering the thousands of miles away the fleet was, Drake smiled. And this was one of the reasons he was a private eye. He loved having the money to buy or rent the posh Oceanious 3 apartments. Without money he never could have seen great views like this.

Listening to the hum of his holographic computer and the sounds of people in other apartments talk, Drake stood up. Feeling the cold wooden floor under his large feet, he hadn't realised it had been so long since he stood up. The floor was nice and warm when he sat down.

Walking on the spot, Drake knew he looked like an idiot but he needed to keep himself moving. He didn't want to be ninety-five with bad joints. Thankfully there was at least sixty years before that, but he might as well help himself now.

As he looked around the dark bedroom of his apartment, he cocked his head at the perfectly arranged bed in the middle of the room with the smooth grey walls. And a built-in wardrobe in the furthest wall. Drake didn't know who loved that feature more, him or his boyfriend Rubio.

Drake missed Rubio a lot. All he wanted to do was snuggle into him and put his fingers through Rubio's short blond hair. But Drake wanted to kick himself as he thought about how he had insisted

Rubio not arrive til tomorrow night.

He didn't wish that now.

Giving himself a final stretch, Drake turned back to his holographic computer and he really couldn't be asked to go back on it.

Drake could hear that snobby client now. Demanding Drake to continue working to dawn. He seriously shook his head at that thought.

If the client found out Drake had gone to bed or wanted to before finding anything exciting, he would just tell them unlike the Iron Priests of Mars, normal people have to sleep.

Deciding to pace around the bedroom, Drake tried to remember what he had found out today about the company (Oceans Travels) the Iron Priests were investigating or wanting to learn about.

On a personal note, Drake had no idea why Mars was interested in a little company that made posh, expensive shuttles for the rich and famous. But in all honesty, if Drake could afford not to work for Mars he could. He remembered from his Navy days how arrogant and snobby they were.

Then Drake smiled as he remembered how Mars couldn't handle the idea of money. Which he laughed at when he asked for twenty thousand credits and they agreed like it was nothing. That's how silly Mars was in reality.

Breathing in the cool slightly peanutty air of the apartment, Drake wondered how best to find out more about the company. An internet deep dive hadn't turned up anything Drake didn't know. The company was rich, couldn't care less about the environment or the Emperor, (Which surprised Drake a little) and they're only concern was a profit.

If Mars wanted a company to buy he could think of at least another three that were a lot better. Oceans Travels felt off. No company that promoted anti-Emperor posts and content would have survived this long without a good reason.

Drake remembered his days in the Navy including some Navy battles with some corporate ships that defied the Emperor. The Human Empire did not tolerate hate against the Glorious Emperor. It was that simple. Drake knew that. Everyone knew that.

Looking back at his holographic computer, Drake's eyes narrowed on the search he had done before he had to take a break. It was a little search on rumours about the company from other businesses. A lot of the time the rumours were just that or lies. But sometimes they were useful.

This time they were interesting.

Drake sat back down on his soft cushioned chair as he read the search results. It seemed a lot of people claimed the company had tights to the Arbiters and other legal organisations connected to the Emperor. That didn't concern Drake that was way above his pay grade.

Then Drake's eyebrows rose as he read another

rumour claiming Oceans Travels had a sorted reputation in the shuttle community.

Leaning back Drake looked back up and admired the stunning ships as he thought about that. It didn't make sense. If their reputation was sorted, then why did so many rich people buy from them?

Opening a new window on his computer, Drake typed in a name of one of his old Navy friends. A Mr Georgious Omega. Drake instantly smiled when he saw Omega was on the planet and not too far away. If anyone would know more about Oceans Travels if it would be the person in charge of licensing commercial travel in the system.

Drake needed to meet him.

\*\*\*

After failing to find anything of note on Oceans Travels, Drake knew he had to call Georgious Omega. Surprisingly enough, Omega wanted to meet up with Drake and catch up. Of course, Drake really didn't want to catch up. He didn't want to hear about the high life of his friend. He only wanted information.

Watching the massive rectangular trucks fly past with their massive red, blue and pink signs and flashing lights zooming past, Drake admired the stunning view of the city from tens of miles above sea level.

Looking down on the city, Drake was surprised to see so many grey shard-like skyscrapers look like toothpicks from up here. With the vehicles, people and cargo travelling to the intergalactic stations in high orbit.

A part of Drake wondered where these trucks would end up. A battlefield? A warzone? Earth? Drake didn't know but it was fun to think about.

The sound of posh snobby rich people laughing fakely made Drake return his attention back to the large open grey platform he was on. With some stunning exotic bright flowers lining the edges along with tens of tables with sweet pastries and freshly green cuboid buns on.

Drake was a bit scared to taste the buns because they did look a bit... adventurous. It was probably their bright sickly green colour but Drake was always up for some adventure.

Placing one of the soft buns in his mouth, Drake instantly smiled as his mouth was full of the sweet syrupy taste of fresh fruits. And not the horrible artificial stuff you normally get. Maybe he needed to bring beautiful Rubio here.

Looking around the café, Drake gave a subtle frown as he saw one couple sitting at a table at the far side. He wasn't exactly sure what they were. Drake supposed they could be human but all their arms, legs and eyes were robotic.

If this person was on the street, Drake would have no doubt they were a military veteran. But with all the customers here being a rich posh people who wouldn't know how to defend themselves even if their life depended on it. Drake guessed that couple just wanted to burn some money.

The tapping of heavy footsteps from metal boots made Drake stand up as he nodded to his friend Georgious Omega. A part of Drake was surprised by his friend. He had certainly lost a lot of weight since their military service days. Omega's skin and face were sharp and rough. Nothing like the arguably attractive stylish face and healthy skin Drake remembered.

Drake offered him a green bun as Omega sat down. Omega eyed him wearily.

"It is good to see you old boy. Been up to much. I've been playing poker with the Commanders personally. Jolly good chaps," Georgious Omega said.

Drake instantly remembered why he had avoided his old friend.

"I'm afraid-"

"Oh come on old chap. I know you're a Private Eye. It's a jolly good shame. We could you a man like you in the service. I know a wonderful little-"

"Thank you Georgious. I mean it. But I am working on the behalf of the Emperor this time in a way. Mars needs information on Oceans Travels,"

"Oh chappy, if Mars wants something I better help you. It's a jolly good shame you're working for Mars. Very strange chaps. Aren't they?"

Drake took a deep breath. "I know they're anti-Emperor. There's a rumour going round they're connected to the Arbiters and their reputation is sorted,"

"Oh yes, Heron. Very sorted. Me and the boys from the shipping Department. Oh, been after them for years. Very dodgy,"

Drake smiled as he offered Omega another bright green bun. Omega looked like he was considering it. He waved Drake's offer away.

"Is there anything concrete? You know how Mars only likes concrete evidence and facts,"

"Um. Come on old chap, you're a clever man. You must have some idea for yourself. I can confirm their connection to the Arbiters,"

Drake leant forward. "Really? What would the Arbiters want with a shuttle making company?"

"Oh Heron, it's actually very clever, very clever. They wanted the company to become drug traffickers so they catch the gang flooding the solar system,"

Drake leant back and took a bite out of those wonderful bright green buns. He loved the taste of that rich fruity syrup.

"Did they catch the gang?" Drake asked.

"Oh yes, it was a jolly good showdown. Very efficient. I think the Glorious Emperor would be proud of my men,"

"Your men?"

"Oh yes, Heron. It was a joint operation. That gang had been causing trouble for the Shipping Department for years,"

It was when Omega said that, Drake started to

wonder what if the so-called shipping department wasn't just for licensing. Drake wanted to ask more but he wasn't sure how to ask carefully.

"Was there anything odd about the operation?"

Omega paused. "Oh yes old boy, there was something very strange actually. Oh you're very clever. There was a shipment of two kilograms of drugs missing. Those damned criminals said it was there. But when Oceans Travels dropped off the ship and drugs it was gone,"

Drake leant in very closely. He could see his payment coming into his account now.

"Final question, was there evidence the Oceans Travels company stole the drugs?"

Georgious Omega leant in close as well.

"Well old chap, there was a suspicious and one of my clever lads. He's very clever lad. He managed to get a transcript from within the company talking about the 2 kilograms of drugs. I'll send it to you now,"

Watching Omega get out his holographic phone and swipe and tap it multiple times, Drake couldn't help but nod his head. Despite the weirdness of the entire thing. Like Mars being interested in a tiny shuttle making company. He had succeeded in finding dirt and hopefully this would help Mars with whatever they needed.

For some reason a little voice popped into Drake's head about not telling Mars what he had found. There was just something about Mars and how cloak and dagger this all seemed. Drake always had his clients tell him what dirt they needed exactly and most of the time why. But this felt different.

Drake didn't know why but he had dealt with Mars and the Martian government twice before. The first time he had been called a *Simple Minded Foolish Human*. Just because he asked how a particular advance machine worked.

The second time was even worse, Drake laughed as he recalled the memory as his Naval ship burning and the Martian Priest with him left him for dead.

All in all Drake couldn't blame himself for being nervous. But he was a Private Eye first and foremost (well he loved Rubio first and foremost). Drake rolled his eyes as he realised he would have to tell Mars what he found. He needed to get paid after all. But maybe he could add a condition first.

"Well done Heron. It's been a jolly good time meeting you again. It would be my pleasure to host you for dinner tonight. It would be bloody marvellous," Georgious Omega said.

"Sorry Omega. Boyfriend's coming planet side tonight,"

"Oh chappy, that is perfectly fine. One more mouth will be perfect. I'll get his shuttle changed and it will drop him off at mine. It's no bother really. See you tonight," Omega said, walking off before Drake could protest.

Drake's mouth dropped as he thought about how

he was going to tell his beautiful Rubio about their dinner plans.

***

Standing on the warm busy spaceport platform with hundreds of people rushing around each second, Drake leant on a metal beam that supported the rather wonderful blue stained glass roof.

It was very beautiful actually.

Watching the other people in their suits, tourist clothes and everything in between rush past, Drake just stood there as he watched the various tubes of grey and black living metal arrive at the spaceport. Dropping off hundreds of passengers every five minutes.

A part of Drake just wished to watch the living metal move and swirl around each other. But he had something far more important to do first.

Breathing in the sweet perfumed (but very artificial air), Drake pressed a little black device in his ear and all the surrounding sounds of people went silent.

"I wasn't expecting you to call on this secure channel," an elderly half mechanical voice said.

"I have done your job for you. I'll have my money now please,"

"Heron, you need to tell me the dirt first. My Masters need that information. The company is... of interest to our purpose,"

"I thought the Martian Government was loyal to

the Glorious Emperor on Earth. That is your purpose as it is for all of us. Serving him is the purpose of Humankind," Drake said, recalling his military days.

"Of course Mr Drake. Mars is loyal only to Earth. But the company is interesting to us. We need the information please,"

Drake paused. Something felt so wrong here, but he needed the money and as a Private Eye he did have a duty to his client. Yet he still had a conscience.

"Tell me why Oceans Travels is interesting to Mars. I'll throw in another piece of information free of charge,"

The woman stopped for a moment. Drake wondered if she was trying to calculate the risk. Mars did love calculations.

"My Masters would probably find that acceptable. Oceans Travels knows of crucial trade routes that the Human Empire relies on. If Mars knows them then we can... help humanity,"

Drake was really getting disturbed by the use of Mars and not Earth, the Emperor or any other term governments normally used.

He just wanted to get this over with. "Oceans Travels has stolen two kilograms of highly illegal drugs in the past. I'll send you the transcript and evidence now,"

Drake could tell the woman was smiling on the other side of the device. Her metal enhancements were whirling strangely. Drake wanted this conversation to end.

"Mr Drake, your payment has been transferred in full, but you mentioned a free piece of information,"

"Their reputation is heavily sorted. I'm sure Mars would use that. Personally I would check out their use of labour. Something doesn't feel right about that," Drake said.

He was about to hang up when the elderly woman said something.

"I was told to say Sarah Oddballa sends her regards,"

The line went dead and the sounds of people talking on the spaceport platform returned.

Drake's mouth dropped a little bit at the name. *Sarah Oddballa.* Drake didn't know how that strange, mysterious woman from an assignment months ago was connected to this. But somehow she was. It was strange, so strange.

Whilst a part of him knew he had probably committed a crime against his Emperor, Drake forced himself to smile and think of all this as tomorrow's problem.

And anyway, Drake knew he had done right as a Private Eye, he had served his client and gotten paid. Exactly like a Private Eye should, whether he did right by doing what he did with the information. He wasn't sure. But right now, he had a very attractive boyfriend to meet.

## A CHEATING AFFAIR

"The heart wants what the heart wants, no matter the price,"

-Old Earth Saying, Pre-Emperor Era

Watching a couple of teenagers exit through the large glass door hand in hand, Drake wondered what his amazing boyfriend Rubio would be doing or saying to him right now. Would Rubio be holding his hand? Or would Rubio want to be acting casual?

Admiring the little metal walls playing holographic films on each of the little black metal diner tables, Drake realised he had missed this simple place whilst he had been travelling the galaxy. Travelling fixing other people's problems.

This little café was a nice reminder of the good old days before he became a Private Eye. Drake nodded as he realised those days were a lot simpler.

Breathing in the freshly brewed coffee from Pluto, Drake remembered how much he loved it in here on Earth. It had been a good decade or two since Drake had been on the birth world of humanity. But it felt great to be back.

Hearing the hissing of machines and ovens and the humming of holograms and other advanced technologies, Drake didn't know he had missed these simple sounds. The year of travelling with Rubio from their last assignment in the galactic east to Earth had taken way too long.

A part of Drake missed the constant background noise of the ship's engines, but as a short woman walked in and a burst of fresh air whipped past him. Drake knew for a fact all this fresh air was far better.

Turning his attention to the little black metal table in front of him, Drake ran his fingers over its smooth surface. Then he picked up a large blue mug of piping hot black coffee. His mouth was instantly filled with the sweet bitter notes of the Plutonian coffee. He loved it.

Yet for some reason, Drake frowned as he wished Rubio was here with him. He wanted a proper date with his boyfriend now they were back on Earth.

But Drake shook his head as he remembered the written request (on actual paper!) for a wealthy woman to meet him and hire him to investigate something.

Drake had no idea how the woman had heard of him. He didn't even know the name, but after a quick internet deep dive, Drake was surprised to learn she was a leading Politician on Earth. *Madame Asche* was her name. There were even rumours of her being nominated for a seat on the Emperor's Council.

A part of Drake wished he could have a major say in the running and fate of the Human Empire. Then he shuttered as he thought about all those hundreds of trillions of lives you would be responsible for. Maybe he didn't want it after all.

Drake stared into the black abyss of his coffee as he felt like something was strange about how the politician found him. He wasn't the most famous Private Eye in the Human Empire. There must have been hundreds of other Private Eyes she could have called.

Certainly she could have called Private Eyes from Earth and save herself the million credits she paid Drake to simply ship him and his boyfriend here. Drake couldn't place his finger on it, but something felt off.

Another wonderful burst of fresh air washed over Drake as a tall woman in a long stylish black coat walked in. She walked over to Drake.

Drake instantly recognised her from the pictures and holographic posters all over the district as the politician. For a politician, he was amazed how thin and healthy she looked. And her sharp angular face and amazing skin must have made all the straight men chase after her.

Drake nodded to her. "Madame Asche, it is an honour to meet you,"

"The pleasure is all mine, Mr Drake. Please know

I very much appreciate your haste in coming to my aid. Please tell Rubio I am sorry for dragging you both into this,"

Drake wasn't sure how diplomatic or informal he should be. He loved being informal with clients. It made them feel like they could trust him, but Drake hadn't worked for a person this powerful before.

"It's fine Madame. Rubio loved the idea of coming to Earth. The birth cradle of Humanity,"

"He has good taste Mr Drake. Earth is a wonderous place. Deadly. But it can be wonderous. I must give you both a private tour of the Emperor's Palace at some point,"

Drake's mouth dropped.

"Mr Drake, I presume you wish to know why I requested your presence,"

Drake managed to regain some type of composure and nodded (and close his mouth).

Madame Asche looked around and leant closer to Drake.

"Mr Drake, I'm sure you're aware there's a rumour going round I could be nominated for a seat on the Emperor's Council. The rumour was confirmed late last night. I guessed this would happen so I summoned you a year ago,"

If this was a normal person, Drake would have no problem calling this client a liar. But as Drake looked at her and soon that innocent looking face. He was fairly sure this woman was not overly innocent. Drake was certain she was a good woman, but extremely calculating.

Drake smiled. "Congratulations. Please call me Heron. Why call me?

"Mr... Heron, I strongly believe my husband is cheating on me. He has probably been doing this for at least fourteen months. I didn't care before my nomination, but this is a threat,"

Drake nodded. "How do you know?"

"Heron, I was a former Intelligence Operative in the Guard before I became a politician. I know the signs. Secret texts. Communications at odd hours. Going missing for minutes or hours at a time. I would have ordered the kill shot if I was still in the military,"

Drake could only nod at her comments. Even in the Navy, he had had to deal with his fair share of traitors. She had a point. In the Emperor's quest to protect humanity, there could be no delay or doubt when it came to traitors.

Picking up his lukewarm blue cup of coffee, Drake took another amazing sip of the wonderful drink.

"Interesting. Do you know who with? Any possible suspects?"

Madame Asche leant in even closer. "I do believe so, Drake. It must be someone from work. He's a Lord Arbiter you see,"

Drake rolled his eyes. Of course the husband had to be a high-ranking law enforcement official. Drake knew he had to be careful.

"Do you have proof? I know Lord Arbiters work with a lot of people,"

Asche smiled and leant back. Taking a large black dataslate out of her coat pocket. She passed it to Drake. It felt strangely cold in his fingers.

"My friend said to bring his laptop in case you wanted to see it,"

Drake's eyes narrowed. "Your friend?"

"Yes Heron, she recommended you to me. She knew I needed to find a Private Eye,"

Drake slowly nodded and asked out of sheer curiosity.

"May I ask her name please?"

Asche paused before saying: "Haras. Do you know her?"

Drake shook his head as he swiped the dataslate. It showed up with his password protected screen. Taking out a small box-like scanner, he pressed it and it unlocked the screen. Madame Asche gasped.

"It seems your husband had a number of meetings every week at the same time," Drake said, looking at the husband's calendar.

"It's nothing. I've checked all that. The appointments all check out. But I was hoping for another set of eyes,"

Drake had to agree with her. He knew most of these names on the calendar. They were all other high ranking Officials or court cases. News of these cases and ruling had even reached other systems in the Empire. Drake shook his head. He needed to find something.

As he started to look through the documents and downloads on the dataslate, he noticed Asche was looking around. He hurried up his search.

"How did you come into politics?" Drake asked, hoping to relax the politician.

She smiled. "As I said I was an intelligence officer but I saw too many corrupt officials on other planets so I wanted to make a change. I swapped my gun for robes and got elected by my district when I returned,"

Drake nodded as he remembered all the corruption he had seen in his military days. Madame Asche looked around once more.

"I'm sorry but there's nothing here," Drake said passing back the dataslate.

Asche frowned.

"Where did you say he worked?" Drake asked.

"His work won't be useful Heron. He has a 'private' office in the far west of this District. I'll send you the coordinates," Madame Asche said, taking out her red holographic phone.

Drake wondered how best to deal with this husband. He had to be careful. He doubted he had too many powerful friends left from his military days to get him out of trouble if he was caught.

"Done. What do I owe you Mr Drake for the completed service?"

"Nothing, Madame. All I wish is that private tour

of the Emperor's Palace with my boyfriend afterwards and I'm allowed to take tourist pictures,"

Asche smiled. "You have yourself a deal Mr Drake,"

\*\*\*

Drake blended into the rest of the tens upon tens of tourists and other business workers on the massive black iron bridge that ran next to the husband's private office.

So many people in all their different clothes from many different regions and planets and systems walked past. Some took pictures of the stunning earth architecture (including some wonderful gothic cathedrals from ancient Earth).

Other people stopped on the bridge and Drake couldn't blame them for looking down over the edge. It was amazing. They were thousands of metres above the ground. It was a stunning piece of Empire engineering.

But the only major problem Drake had ever with tourists was their... unique smells. A lot of these people probably came from normal worlds, where people wore perfumes. Drake loved the smell of the sweet, flowery perfumes. But he much preferred the hot guys walking about with their manly aftershaves. They reminded him of his beautiful Rubio with his stunning aftershave and... he was just perfect.

Drake frowned as he realised other people must have come from ecclesiastical worlds dedicated to the so-called (and false idea) of the God Emperor of the

Human Empire. Breathing in their awful holy oils and all their other foul smelling chemicals Drake remembered why he never did business on these worlds.

Listening to the talking of the tourists and the hum of the machines inside the bridge and the other skyscrapers nearby, Drake slowly turned around and got out his touristy big camera and looked at the massive office in front of him.

Drake had to admit it was a pretty clever place of a private office because it looked like just another massive glass skyscraper. Home to one to the millions if not billions of companies on Earth. That's if the tourists didn't think it belonged to one of the Emperor's departments.

Zooming in with his camera, Drake nodded as he realised how perfect the whole thing was. Only tourists walked across the bridge and the odd business person who did walk wouldn't focus on yet another massive corporate building. It was literally hiding in plain sight. Clever. Very clever.

Knowing if anyone looked, it would look like he was just looking through pictures on his camera, Drake focused on the large yellow desk in the office.

A part of Drake wondered if the desk was effective at all. It was large but it was completely covered in piles of dataslates. Most of them were probably legal reports, but Drake focused on the person sitting in a small black chair behind the desk.

Getting a clear visual of the desk, Drake gave an involuntarily smile as he noticed the Husband. Asche definitely had good taste in men, but in his baggy suit and short salt and pepper hair with a slim build. The Husband lacked Rubio's beauty a lot.

Scanning the office with his camera, Drake wanted to see some kind of sign of an affair. Some female clothes. A toothbrush. A knocked over pile of documents.

Nothing.

Drake rolled his eyes as he thought about how much longer was it going to be until the woman came.

Remembering what Madame Asche had texted him almost as soon as they left the café. She said her husband was meant to be working late tonight at his main office. Not his private office. Sadly a little lie like that was hardly evidence for a divorce.

After a few moments, the Husband stood up and pushed his chair away. It hit the wall. Drake took a few pictures. But as he scanned the office with his camera he couldn't see anyone. There was no one there.

Returning his focus on the Husband, it looked like he was making out with someone.

Drake zoomed in.

When the camera reached the maximum, Drake could see everything about the Husband. He could see every hair on his beard, every eyebrow rise rising and even blood rushing to every… bad place.

But there was no one there.

Taking a step back Drake tried to understand what was going on, he could clearly see the Husband was making out with someone. But there was no one there. His camera couldn't see it. Even if Drake tried to strain his eyes he couldn't see anyone.

What was going on?

Pressing his weight against the warm railings of the bridge, Drake tried to remember his military days. Maybe there was some sort of device that made a person invisible. But if that was true how could the husband see the woman. It was strange.

Drake once heard a device that could make a person invisible but that was used by operatives of the Assassins and some other Agents of the Emperor.

Seeing a woman out of the corner of his eye lean against the edge of the bridge, Drake looked at them quickly. But he stared at them the second he looked at this woman.

He knew there was something familiar about her. Her smooth middle aged (or well preserved) skin and her long grey hair. There was something familiar. But most importantly the woman wore a long sweeping bright red dress. Drake was sure straight people would have found the woman attractive. But he knew she was dangerous.

Drake smiled. "Haras. Clever. An anagram I presume?"

"Now, now Mr Drake. I know I've changed my

appearance a little but I am still known to you as Sarah Oddballa," the woman said, her voice soft, matter of fact but there was an edge of authority to it.

Drake smiled as soon as he heard the name. He had no idea how this mysterious woman was connected to this random cheating case. He had only met her once on an assignment two years ago, but this woman was dangerous.

"How are you involved in my case? Why did you want the Madame Asche to hire me?"

"Mr Drake, you know I work in mysterious ways. I wanted to see you again. Watch him," Sarah said, pointing to the husband in the office, who was still making out with no one.

Drake was about to say something before he realised the true purpose of her meeting him.

"You aren't here, are you? The Husband must believe he's making out with a real person. Like I believe you're here. What did you do?"

Sarah's eyes widened. "Mr Drake, you are very clever. Extremely clever. It's a new piece of technology available to only my organisation. Don't feel bad. This is fun,"

So many questions were flying through Drake's mind at that moment. But he only wanted to ask one.

"Is there a particular outcome you wanted?"

Sarah smiled and nodded. "Mr Drake when we met two years ago I was impressed. You are a good man. Very rare in my line of work to meet a good man. So I wanted to give you something,"

Drake took a step away. "I don't believe you. You wouldn't become friends with a leading politician just for me... Unless you want to buy me favour for the future,"

Again Sarah nodded. "Of course Mr Drake, you will be useful to me in the future. I just don't want you to forget me,"

"That won't be hard,"

Sarah gave a short laugh. "Check your camera you should have the pictures you need by now. Good Day Mr Drake. Until we meet again,"

Checking his camera, Drake flicked through some of the pictures and he shook his head as he saw all the pictures he had taken without the woman. Now were filled with explicit pictures of the husband making out with the woman. It was strange.

A small part of Drake didn't want to show Madame Asche these photos. He wanted, needed to get natural photos. Drake didn't want to be a pawn in the mysterious Sarah Oddballa's game. But time was money and these photos got him this money.

Drake frowned as he needed to decide what did his heart want. The money or natural photos that proved his skill as a Private Eye?

\*\*\*

Sending off his written report to Madame Asche, Drake sat down on his apartment's large bright purple bed with the soft velvety sheets touching his skin.

Laying on his back, Drake looked up at the

bright white ceiling and ignored the even brighter white walls and simply wondered about this case.

Breathing in the fresh air from the air conditioning, Drake couldn't understand what this was all about. He knew Sarah wasn't the type to care about a person. She couldn't have cared if he got paid, which he wouldn't.

Then it hit him.

Listening to the muttering of other people through walls, Drake smiled as he wondered if Sarah wanted him and Rubio to get access to the Palace.

If Sarah could hack into his camera and upload photos, then would it be difficult to do something if he was inside the Palace? Maybe she planted a device on him or Rubio that would activate once past Palace security.

Was he risking the Human Empire by going on a tour?

Maybe this was what his choice actually was. Drake nodded at that idea. Of course this was his real choice. He knew Sarah probably convinced Madame Asche to offer up the Palace tour as a reward knowing it was too good of an opportunity to waste.

Shaking his head and loving the sweet fresh air as he breathed it in, Drake couldn't believe he was actually going to message Madame Asche and politely request credits instead of a tour.

Or maybe that's what Sarah wanted. Drake laughed to himself as he wondered about her plan. Maybe her plan was to make the Madame Asche have less money. It would make sense. A divorce was expensive.

Smiling to himself, Drake made the most weirdest decision of his life. He picked up his holographic phone and messaged Madame Asche. *No Payment Required.*

Drake knew it was a bad decision but he didn't need the money. And that decision was still in the interest of his business. Drake cocked his head at that thought. But he knew he was right. That decision didn't cost him much money because the entire job only took about six hours. It probably made him a political friend too.

Drake gave a massive smile as he realised the final thing his decision granted him. It made Sarah's plans fail. He was sure on that.

Nodding to himself, Drake knew at the end of the day he had done right and followed his heart. No matter the money it costed him, Drake was certain he had helped his Human Empire today.

But most importantly, he now had the rest of the evening to spend with his beautiful Rubio and play with his stunning short blond hair.

The sound of the door of the apartment opening made Drake jump up. His Rubio was here and this job was done.

# THE LITTLE CAFÉ AFFAIR

"Buying A Company is Never Easy. Always Be Careful or You Will Be Bitten,"

-Old Business Saying, Unknown Planet

Some people might have called Heron Drake, Private Eye, a risk taker but he didn't agree. This was all part of the fun.

Taking a sip of the sweet, black strong coffee, Drake almost smiled as his mouth was filled with the amazing tastes of fruit and sweet delicious honey. This café knew how to make a great cup of coffee.

Drake looked at his holographic computer screen filled with banking documents and other confidential pieces of information. As he listened to the other customers talk and moan about how wonderful the food was.

He had to admit the customers made great points and now he was really attempted to buy one of those amazing sweet sticky buns everyone was talking about.

Maybe later.

Looking at the small red plastic table he sat at, Drake felt the soft, inviting cushioned chair mould to his body as he moved slightly. The café was great at a lot of things clearly but Drake was here for a very particular purpose.

Carefully focusing on the little red café with its bright red plastic tables and red cups and plates that everyone was happily eating from. Drake didn't see anything to give him a cause for concern.

But this wasn't right.

Turning his attention back to his holographic computer, Drake circled the perfect amount of money the financial records showed.

Remembering what his client had said about researching the little café to see if it was a wise investment for a large company, Drake felt something was very off.

He had worked for hundreds of investment companies to check investments before. But never had these companies that were the investment had such perfect records. It was all too easy to class something as a business expense when it legally wasn't.

None of that here. These records were too perfect.

Looking at some of the other transactions and records he had been given by the insurance company, Drake reran his calculations and his assessment of the little café.

Again it was perfect. Not a single zero in the wrong place. No cheeky boss trying to take a few credits. Nothing.

Smiling to a waiter as he passed, Drake tried to think about what to do. The records were clearly faked and there was something else. The little café didn't feel as rich as the records were making it out to be.

And that's why Drake wanted to be here. Of course, he knew for a fact it was ballsy and bold to come to the little café and check their records in public. But Drake needed to be here for the staff.

A part of Drake wished his boyfriend Rubio was here but Drake had wanted to deal with this alone. At first he thought it would only take a few hours, now Drake was sadly thinking it would be longer. He hated telling Rubio to do other things. He had to stop doing that.

With a short, thin female waitress in a tight black dress walking towards him, Drake waved at her and she walked over. She was probably no older than 20.

"Hello Sir, is there anything I can get you? A coffee? One of our famous sticky buns?" she asked.

Drake looked around, no one was watching and leant a little closer.

"Excuse me, how long have you worked here?" Drake asked.

"Sir, I've worked here for five years since Septemious,"

"Then you know about the financial situation the café is in,"

The waitress nodded. "Who are you?"

"I am Mr Blake, a man from Head Office,"

The woman paused and clearly didn't know the little café didn't have a Head Office as she nodded.

Drake smiled and subtly gave her a hundred credits.

"I need to know where all the money from the café goes,"

The waitress looked around. No one was watching.

"Mr Blake. I can't,"

Drake looked at the hundred credits in her hand.

"Fine Mr Blake. I cannot tell you for legal reasons. But there's a woman who might be able to help you,"

Drake leant forward. "Who?"

A tall muscular man in a tight black t-shirt walked towards Drake.

"And I'll get you your bill for you, kind Sir. Thank you for eating at the Little Café today," the Waitress said, walking away.

The muscular man smiled at Drake. Probably the manager but Drake frowned. He needed that lead. All the financial records were too clean to give them any leads.

Drake cocked his head at that idea. He could (he supposed) go down to the Planet's Company House and look through all the records to see who submitted them to the Government. That would tell him who submitted the false records. But that would take months.

"And here's your bill, Kind Sir. Have a great day," the waitress said as she walked away.

Opening up the small holographic wallet, Drake almost frowned but made sure he didn't. He was surprised to see the Waitress had paid for his bill but there was a name inside. *Ellender Basic*.

Drake's eyebrows rose as he remembered where he had heard the name before. She was a high powered tech entrepreneur. He remembered Rubio talking about her, as she's trying to get a contract with the Central Government on Earth.

Drake didn't know how she was connected, but he had to find out.

\*\*\*

Drake didn't know whether to be more surprised at the choice of her meeting place or the fact it had taken him three hours to talk to her assistant.

Not being entirely impressed, Drake frowned as he looked around the large open plan restaurant where Ellender had chosen to meet him.

Drake supposed the restaurant was okay. He didn't like the open plan concept. From the far corner he was sitting on with a small golden table in front of him, Drake could see the entire place. He could even see the holographic door on the other side of the restaurant.

Drake's stomach tightened into a knot as he watched the other people sitting at nearby and far away tables eating all sorts of delights. All the rich and wealthy of the Human Empire was here. Some were judges, some were Lord Commanders and some were war heroes.

Breathing in the amazing air of the restaurant, Drake couldn't believe how brilliant this place was. He loved the smell of the fresh juicy meats and the strong smells of cinnamon and lemon from a dessert on a nearby table.

It made his mouth water and fill with the tastes of sweet black apple pie his mother use to make back on Earth.

It was amazing.

Drake didn't want to leave. Especially, as he smiled at the crackling, bubbling sound of the Space Pigs roasting and bright blue meat being thrown into the oven.

He couldn't wait to eat. Before he left this planet, Drake was definitely going to bring his beautiful Rubio here.

Seeing the holographic door open, Drake prepared himself as he saw a tall slim woman wearing a stunning long black dress with six-inch heels walk into the restaurant and walk towards Drake.

Drake was a bit surprised by her long blond hair. He had no doubt straight men would fall all over her and would do anything for her. That's the last thing that would work on Drake. He smiled at that.

As she elegantly took her seat, Ellender gave Drake a large movie star smile. Drake noticed lots of the men in the restaurant were staring at her. Their mouths open.

"Mr Drake, do not look at those other men. If they try anything on me, I will deal with them," Ellender said, her voice somehow managing to make that not sound threatening.

"Thank you for meeting with me. I know you must be busy,"

"It is no problem, Heron. May I call you Heron?"

Drake nodded.

"Excellent. Heron, what do you wish to talk about that was so urgent?"

"The Little Café. Do you know of it?"

Ellender smiled and picked up the menu. Her eyes scanning it carefully like her life depended on choosing the right thing.

"Is it the records you're asking about?"

Drake picked up his own menu. "Yes. How do you know? Please tell me you're not the company looking to invest. That would be embarrassing,"

Her smile deepened. "No, Heron. Rest assured I am not the investing company but I would deter anyone from doing so,"

Drake placed the menu back down. "Why?"

"You saw the records Heron. You know they're faked and you wouldn't have called me unless there was more,"

"A waitress there said you know something about where the missing money's going,"

Ellender looked up at the ceiling before slowly looking back at Drake.

"Heron, I am sorry but you've wasted your time. I cannot legally tell you,"

Drake looked back at the menu. "That's what the waitress said. I'm guessing Non-disclosure agreement,"

The woman nodded and her eyes turned watery.

"It's how you got the money to start your tech company, isn't it?"

Ellender slowly said. "You're. Very clever. Mr Drake,"

Drake wanted to rub her hand to reassure her that she was safe but he didn't. It didn't seem the place.

"I know you can't tell me or even confirm the… *interfering* happened. But is there anything concrete I can give my client?"

She shook her head.

Drake put down the menu and looked at her.

"Why did the waitress want me to see you? She could have told me all this herself,"

Ellender shrugged.

Drake before having an idea.

"What's the price for breaking the non-disclosure agreement?"

Ellender put her own menu down and grinned.

"Two million credits. Your waitress is a clever girl. I can afford that if needed,"

Drake paused. Two million credits was a lot of money but surely stopping the money disappearing, that was probably being used to pay off girls, was more important. He had to be loyal to his client.

Ellender got out her large black holographic phone and swiped it a few times.

"What you doing?" Drake asked.

"When it first happened, I recorded a video of myself talking about it. I recorded some of my injuries too,"

Drake leant forward.

"I'm just going to release it to all the media outlets, and transfer the two million credits,"

Drake nodded.

"Done,"

Drake smiled as he could feel the payment flowing into his bank account from the insurance company. But he smiled even more because he could literally see Ellender become stronger and more relaxed. Like a massive weight had been lifted off.

"Thank you for that Mr Drake. I hope that satisfies you,"

"Yes it does. Mrs Basic,"

Ellender picked up the menu and looked at Drake.

"Come on Heron, we need to celebrate. You must try the Luminous Oysters from the Luminous

System. They are wonderful,"

Drake laughed to himself as he realised it was going to be an interesting night.

"And Heron, I hear you have friends on Earth. I might need you,"

Drake rolled his eyes and smiled. This meal wasn't going to be free.

\*\*\*

Checking his bank balance and seeing it had increased very nicely, Drake put his blue holographic phone away and sat down on his favourite black soft chair in their temporary apartment.

Drake couldn't put into words how excited he was to see Rubio when he came back from work. Drake smiled at the word *work*, he knew all Rubio was doing was talking to homeless kids. He loved it and Drake sadly knew Rubio would miss it when they left this planet.

Making sure everything was perfect for his beautiful Rubio, Drake looked at the smooth white wooden floors and the smooth walls, with their bright holographic lights and the TV and other entertainment bits safely against the wall.

Drake looked at the two large sofas nearby. He was looking forward to using them later with Rubio!

Breathing in the perfectly cool air and listening to the quiet foot traffic outside, Drake relaxed into his soft chair.

Heron Drake relaxed even more as he remembered how delighted the insurance company had been with Drake's report. He was pretty happy with it too considering the Little Café had folded and the Arbiters had investigated. Revealing over fifty women and twenty men had been abused, and that's before the Arbiters found the drugs and weapons they were selling.

A very good day in Drake's books.

Feeling his phone vibrate, Drake answered it.

"Drake, Private Eye. How may I help you?"

"Mr Drake, it is a pleasure to have you help me again,"

As soon as Drake heard that smooth, matter of fact voice with an edge of authority. He knew exactly who it was. The woman who kept popping up in a handful of his cases from time to time.

"Sarah Oddballa," Drake said.

"Mr Drake, I must thank you. I didn't want to invest and buy the Little Café anyway. I just needed a strong Private Eye like you to investigate,"

Drake smiled at her. She was always so damn clever.

"Don't feel bad Mr Drake. You helped a lot of people get justice today and I've forgiven you for screwing up The Cheating Affair with that Politician,"

Drake smiled for a different reason now. As much as he loved helping that politician, his favourite part of the case was stopping Sarah from getting what she wanted.

"What did you get out of the Little Café? You

never act without there being something in this for you."

"Oh Mr Drake, you are extremely clever. I will give you that but I have to go. The Little Café contained some threats that I needed gone. The abusers needed to be stopped. Be proud of yourself. Until we meet again Mr Drake,"

She cut the line.

Putting his phone away, Drake shook his head as he tried to forget about Sarah Oddballa and her crazy, mysterious schemes.

Then Drake wondered if he needed to remember an old business saying from his youth. Maybe he needed to be careful about buying whatever client gave him their business. After all he had a feeling one day he would get bitten. And the thing about getting bitten is it always hurts, but sometimes it kills.

DRAKE SCIENCE FICTION PRIVATE EYE SHORT
STORIES COLLECTION

**GET YOUR FREE EXCLUSIVE GARRO SHORT STORY HERE!**

https://www.subscribepage.com/garrosignup

Thank you for reading.

I hoped you enjoyed it.

If you want a FREE book and keep up to date about new books and project. Then please sign up for my newsletter at www.connorwhiteley.net/

Have a great day.

## About the author:

Connor Whiteley is the author of over 30 books in the sci-fi fantasy, nonfiction psychology and books for writer's genre and he is a Human Branding Speaker and Consultant.

He is a passionate warhammer 40,000 reader, psychology student and author.

Who narrates his own audiobooks and he hosts The Psychology World Podcast.

All whilst studying Psychology at the University of Kent, England.

Also, he was a former Explorer Scout where he gave a speech to the Maltese President in August 2018 and he attended Prince Charles' 70$^{th}$ Birthday Party at Buckingham Palace in May 2018.

Plus, he is a self-confessed coffee lover!

## OTHER SHORT STORIES BY CONNOR WHITELEY

Blade of The Emperor

Arbiter's Truth

The Bloodied Rose

Asmodia's Wrath

Heart of A Killer

Emissary of Blood

Computation of Battle

Old One's Wrath

Puppets and Masters

Ship of Plague

Interrogation

Sacrifice of the Soul

Heart of The Flesheater

Heart of The Regent

Heart of The Standing

DRAKE SCIENCE FICTION PRIVATE EYE SHORT
STORIES COLLECTION

Feline of The Lost

Heart of The Story

The Family Mailing Affair

Defining Criminality

The Martian Affair

A Cheating Affair

The Little Café Affair

## Other books by Connor Whiteley:

### The Fireheart Fantasy Series

Heart of Fire

Heart of Lies

Heart of Prophecy

Heart of Bones

Heart of Fate

### The Garro Series- Fantasy/Sci-fi

GARRO: GALAXY'S END

GARRO: RISE OF THE ORDER

GARRO: END TIMES

GARRO: SHORT STORIES

GARRO: COLLECTION

GARRO: HERESY

GARRO: FAITHLESS

GARRO: DESTROYER OF WORLDS

GARRO: COLLECTIONS BOOK 4-6

DRAKE SCIENCE FICTION PRIVATE EYE SHORT STORIES COLLECTION

GARRO: MISTRESS OF BLOOD

GARRO: BEACON OF HOPE

GARRO: END OF DAYS

Winter Series- Fantasy Trilogy Books

WINTER'S COMING

WINTER'S HUNT

WINTER'S REVENGE

WINTER'S DISSENSION

Miscellaneous:

THE ANGEL OF RETURN

THE ANGEL OF FREEDOM

## All books in 'An Introductory Series':

BIOLOGICAL PSYCHOLOGY 3$^{RD}$ EDITION

COGNITIVE PSYCHOLOGY THIRD EDITION

SOCIAL PSYCHOLOGY- 3$^{RD}$ EDITION

ABNORMAL PSYCHOLOGY 3$^{RD}$ EDITION

PSYCHOLOGY OF RELATIONSHIPS- 3$^{RD}$ EDITION

DEVELOPMENTAL PSYCHOLOGY 3$^{RD}$ EDITION

HEALTH PSYCHOLOGY

RESEARCH IN PSYCHOLOGY

A GUIDE TO MENTAL HEALTH AND TREATMENT AROUND THE WORLD- A GLOBAL LOOK AT DEPRESSION

FORENSIC PSYCHOLOGY

THE FORENSIC PSYCHOLOGY OF THEFT, BURGLARY AND OTHER

## DRAKE SCIENCE FICTION PRIVATE EYE SHORT STORIES COLLECTION

RIMES AGAINST PROPERTY

CRIMINAL PROFILING: A FORENSIC PSYCHOLOGY GUIDE TO FBI PROFILING AND GEOGRAPHICAL AND STATISTICAL PROFILING.

CLINICAL PSYCHOLOGY

FORMULATION IN PSYCHOTHERAPY

PERSONALITY PSYCHOLOGY AND INDIVIDUAL DIFFERENCES

CLINICAL PSYCHOLOGY REFLECTIONS VOLUME 1

CLINICAL PSYCHOLOGY REFLECTIONS VOLUME 2

www.ingramcontent.com/pod-product-compliance
Lightning Source LLC
LaVergne TN
LVHW011855060526
838200LV00054B/4339